A Tiger Like Me

by Michael Engler

illustrated by Joëlle Tourlonias

translated by Laura Watkinson

amazon crossing kids

When the first ray of sunshine falls on my soft sleeping place,
I yawn and stretch.
I flex my muscles and test my claws.
Calmly and quietly.
Then I fill my lungs with air, and I ROAR

as loud as I can: WOAR!

Because I am a tiger, a wide-awake tiger!

Cold water and slippery soap must never touch my beautiful fur.
And brushes and combs are not good for tigers.
I have to get away from the bathroom!
I need to run!

But Mom is guarding the door—and she blocks my escape route.
So I duck—so sleek, so smooth, so smart—
and I dash past her hands in a flash.

Because I am a tiger,
a superfast tiger!

Tigers always need a good breakfast.
It makes us powerful and strong.
I leap up to my feeding spot.
With my tiger appetite, I devour my tiger flakes
and drink a big glass of blood . . . orange juice!
I crunch and munch just like a tiger.
And then I'm ready for new adventures.

Because I am a tiger, a greedy, gutsy tiger!

My sharp tiger eyes spot a great hiding place,
deep in the depths of the forest.
I sneak into my hideaway as quietly as only a tiger can,
and soon I am invisible.
When Mom comes along, I'll give her a fright.
This is going to be fun!

But then it gets dark—and really, really scary.
This isn't a hideaway. It's a trap!
The trap snaps shut and holds me in its grip.
I shout for help. I wriggle and I struggle.
But that only makes it worse.
Oh no!
Just in time, Tiger-Mom comes to the rescue.
She grabs my paws and pulls me
out of the nasty, biting trap.

Because I am a tiger,
a clumsy, klutzy tiger!

Now I want to go out into the open air.
There's snow on the plains outside!
I pull on my winter tiger coat and my soft tiger hat to warm my ears.
Time to go! Into the snow! Hurray for tiger fun!

Snow sprays out from under my quick tiger paws.
Icicles rattle with my big tiger roars!
My fiery breath turns the air to smoke.
And my tiger tongue
catches snowflakes in midair!

I jump and pounce, I roll and fall,
and I don't hurt myself—not one bit.
Winter is so wonderful for a tiger like me!

Because I am a tiger, a whirling,
swirling tiger!

When my stomach starts to rumble,
I prowl back into the house, looking for food.
I know I'll find some tiger prey in the kitchen . . .
Quietly purring, I lurk in the shadows of the table and chair.
No one can see me now. Then . . .
I jump up onto the chair in a single leap! I look at the table—
and I can't believe my luck!
Right in front of me! It's a great, big, tasty tiger cake.
I smile and flash my teeth.

Because I am a tiger,
a hungry, hungry tiger!

Later I paint my face black and orange and quietly creep up on Dad.
He is hiding behind his newspaper.
He says he needs some peace and quiet.
Tigers don't! Tigers don't like peace and quiet!
So I stalk from door to sofa . . .
I take a very big breath . . .
Then I jump at Dad with a great, big roar!

The newspaper rips. And Dad howls.
His face turns white and then red, as red as a raspberry.
Dad jumps up. He's a hunter now.
He tries to catch me. He wants to trap me.
But his hand just swipes at my tail.
I'm way too fast for him.

Because I am a tiger,
a wild and wary tiger!

He sends me to my room,
but that's fine by me.
I build a den out of chairs and blankets,
where it's soft and dark and safe.
It's a perfect hideaway for tigers.
No one will ever find me!

Because I am a tiger, a clever, cunning tiger.

In the evening, Tiger-Mom, Tiger-Dad, and—of course!—Tiger-Me
are sitting together on the wild carpet
and having so much fun.
We are folding and tying and sticking and painting and cutting,
with scissors and paper and glue,
with pencils and ribbons and clay.
What are we making? What do you think?
Tigers! Tigers! Tigers!

Because I am a tiger, a crafty, creative tiger.

Tigers don't need to brush their teeth.
That's just for human children.
Brushing teeth is bad for tigers!
All that frothing foam—that's not good for fangs.
And tiger paws aren't made to hold toothbrushes.
Plus, tigers can't stand on their two back legs for long.
I shake my head and dig in my claws.

Because I am a tiger, a growling, yowling tiger.

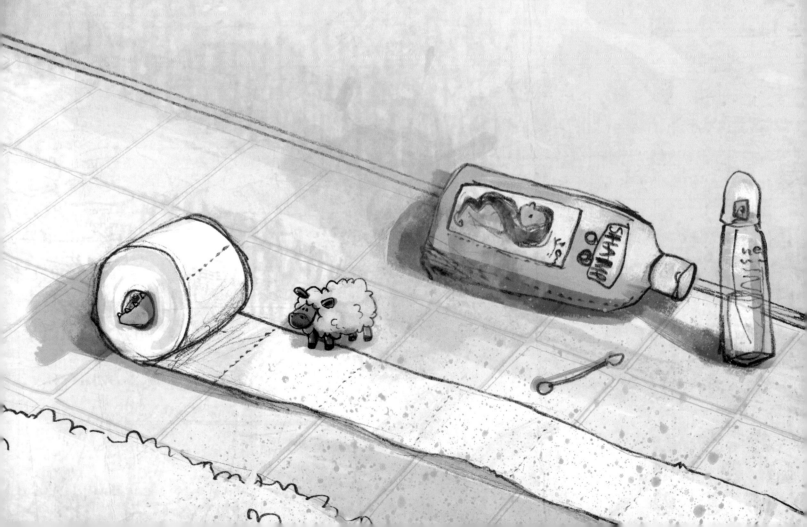

It got dark way too soon today.
I'm still full of tiger zip!
Dad sends me to my sleeping place.
But I'm not sleepy.
My ears are listening, and I'm watching the light in the hallway.
When the floorboards creak and shadows dash across the floor,
when the sheets in the big bedroom rustle,
I know that the best part of my tiger day is here!

Because I am a tiger, a wide-awake tiger.

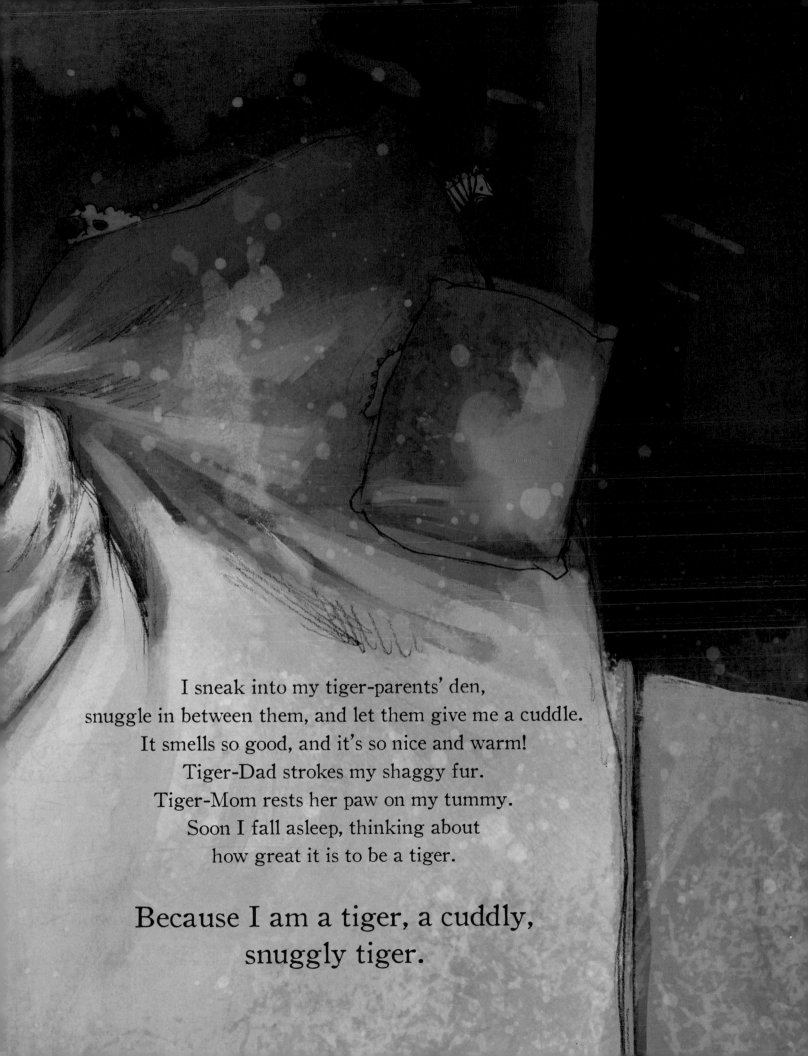

I sneak into my tiger-parents' den,
snuggle in between them, and let them give me a cuddle.
It smells so good, and it's so nice and warm!
Tiger-Dad strokes my shaggy fur.
Tiger-Mom rests her paw on my tummy.
Soon I fall asleep, thinking about
how great it is to be a tiger.

Because I am a tiger, a cuddly,
snuggly tiger.

The tiger returns to his den,
where he lies down, worn out after a long, exciting day.
In the forest and on the plain, everything is finally silent.
The little tiger shuts his eyes and dreams.

Even before the first ray of sunshine lights the sky,
one animal is already stirring.
In the tiger's den, two eyes blink sleepily.
The peaceful night is over.
Because the king of the forest is awake!

Previously published as *Ich bin ein Tiger*
by Annette Betz Verlag in der Ueberreuter
Verlag GmbH in Germany in 2016.
Translated from German by Laura Watkinson.
First published in English by Amazon Crossing Kids
in collaboration with Amazon Crossing in 2019.

Published by Amazon Crossing Kids, New York,
in collaboration with Amazon Crossing

www.apub.com

Amazon, Amazon Crossing, and all related logos are
trademarks of Amazon.com, Inc., or its affiliates.

ISBN-13: 9781542044561 (hardcover)
ISBN-10: 1542044561 (hardcover)

The illustrations are rendered digitally.
Book design by Tanya Ross-Hughes

Printed in China

First Edition

10 9 8 7 6 5 4 3 2 1